The Hound

A Haunting Lovecraftian Horror Tale –
Forbidden Relics and Supernatural
Terror

A Modern Translation

Adapted for the Contemporary Reader

H.P. Lovecraft

Translated by Tim Zengerink

Table of Contents

Preface - Message to the Reader

What If You Could Help Rebuild the Greatest Library in Human History?

Thousands of years ago, the Library of Alexandria stood as the crown jewel of human achievement — a sanctuary where the collected wisdom of every known civilization was gathered, preserved, and shared freely.

And then, it was lost.

Through fire, conquest, and the slow erosion of time, humanity lost not just books — but ideas, dreams, discoveries, and stories that could have changed the world forever.

Today, the Library of Alexandria lives again — and you are invited to be a part of its restoration.

Our mission is simple yet profound:

To rebuild the greatest library the world has ever known, and to translate all timeless works into every language and dialect, so that no seeker of knowledge is ever left behind again.

By joining our movement to rebuild the modern Library of Alexandria, you become part of an unprecedented mission:

- **Unlimited Access to the Greatest Audiobooks & eBooks Ever Written:**

  Instantly explore thousands of legendary works—Plato, Shakespeare, Jane Austen, Leo Tolstoy, and countless more. All instantly available to read or listen, placing a complete literary universe at your fingertips.

- **Beautiful Paperback & Deluxe Editions at Printing Cost**

  Own any title as an elegant paperback, deluxe hardcover, or stunning collectible boxset—offered to you at true printing cost, delivered straight to your door. Build your personal Library of Alexandria, crafted for beauty, built for durability, and worthy of proud display.

- **Fresh Translations for Modern Readers—in Every Language & Dialect**

  Enjoy timeless masterpieces reimagined in clear, contemporary language—no more outdated phrases or obscure references. Alongside the original versions, we're tirelessly translating these classics into every language and dialect imaginable, ensuring accessibility and understanding across cultures and generations.

- **Join a Global Renaissance of Literature & Knowledge**

  You directly support expanding our library, publishing deluxe editions at true cost, translating works into all global languages, and bringing humanity's greatest stories to people everywhere. By joining today, you're not just preserving a legacy of masterpieces; you set in motion a powerful wave of literary accessibility.

Become a Torchbearer of Knowledge.

Join us for free now at **LibraryofAlexandria.com**

Together, we will ensure that the light of human wisdom never fades again.

With gratitude and a shared love of knowledge,

The Modern Library of Alexandria Team

Visit:

www.libraryofalexandria.com

Or scan the code below:

Introduction

Forbidden Aesthetics, Grave Robbing, and the Descent into Madness

Among H.P. Lovecraft's early works, "The Hound" stands out as one of his most lurid, atmospheric, and perversely indulgent tales. Written in September 1922 and first published in Weird Tales in 1924, it is a feverish descent into Gothic decadence and occult horror. Lovecraft himself dismissed it later as "a piece of extravagance," but over time, the story has come to be appreciated not only for its richly decadent tone but also for its foundational role in shaping what would later become key elements of the Cthulhu Mythos. Within its tightly crafted structure and opulent prose lies a striking meditation on obsession, transgression, and the price of violating the sanctity of death.

The story centers on two nameless narrators—eccentric antiquarians who have devoted their lives not to the study of history, but to the aesthetic and psychological pleasure of desecration. Living together in a decaying mansion adorned with relics of death—mummified heads, ancient tomes, and grave goods from around the world—they practice a twisted form of connoisseurship: exhuming the dead for the thrill of possession. These are not thieves driven by greed or occultists driven by metaphysics. They are aesthetes of horror, intoxicated by the power of antiquity and the thrill of desecration.

Their fatal mistake comes when they exhume the grave of a centuries-dead nobleman in a supposedly cursed Dutch cemetery. Among the grave's contents, they discover an amulet inscribed with unknown characters—an object clearly ancient, otherworldly, and resonant with supernatural force. They steal it. And from that moment forward, they are hunted by something invisible, primal, and relentless. Strange noises, howling wind, mutilated bodies, and the sound of vast wings accompany their descent into madness. Their home is invaded, their sleep disturbed, their minds tormented. Eventually, one of them dies, torn apart by something unseen. The narrator, spiraling into insanity, returns to the grave to replace the amulet, hoping to appease the entity that now haunts him. The story ends with his own impending death and the implicit triumph of the ancient horror they had awakened.

On the surface, "The Hound" is a richly stylized Gothic revenge tale. But beneath its decadent surface lies a deeper meditation on the consequences of violating ancient boundaries. Lovecraft does not merely warn against stealing from graves—he warns against stealing from time itself. The amulet is not just a relic. It is a symbol of a deeper order, an ancient balance between the living and the dead that must not be disrupted. The horror that ensues is not arbitrary. It is justice—not in the moral sense, but in the cosmic sense that Lovecraft would come to define: the idea that the universe has laws deeper than human morality, and that to transgress them is to invite destruction.

Aesthetic Horror, Occult Symbolism, and the Birth of the Mythos

"The Hound" occupies a special place in Lovecraft's bibliography because it marks one of the earliest references to the fictional grimoire known as the Necronomicon—a term that would become central to the mythology he would construct over the next decade. In this story, the book is listed casually, almost as an accessory in the characters' museum of death. Yet that single reference plants the seed of a mythos that would grow to encompass entire pantheons of eldritch gods, ancient civilizations, and incomprehensible horrors lurking beyond the veil of time and space. It is through this reference that "The Hound" connects to the larger web of stories that define Lovecraft's mature work.

But the real power of this tale lies not in its contribution to a fictional universe, but in its atmospheric intensity. The story's prose is florid, almost decadent, filled with archaic diction, sensual imagery, and linguistic excess. Critics have often pointed to this style as evidence of Lovecraft's youthful indulgence, but it also serves a critical purpose. The prose reflects the psychology of the protagonists—their intoxication with death, their obsession with the aesthetics of the macabre. Their world is not one of moral consequence, but of sensory experience. They are not afraid of death; they are fascinated by it. They crave its texture, its smell, its artifacts.

This obsession is what ultimately damns them. In Lovecraft's fiction, obsession is a form of madness—a deviation from the natural balance of reason and survival. The protagonists of "The Hound" are not rationalists, nor are they scientists. They are aesthetes who mistake the surface of horror for its substance. They believe they can collect, catalogue, and consume the dead without consequence. But the amulet they steal is not a museum piece. It is an object of power, a key to a system of cosmic balance they do not understand. Their attempt to possess it triggers a response not from a supernatural ghost, but from an ancient, perhaps extradimensional force that defies categorization.

Lovecraft never describes the creature explicitly. We are told only of its sounds, its mutilations, its tracks. This restraint is typical of Lovecraft's technique: the horror is not in what is seen, but in what cannot be seen. The titular hound may or may not be a literal dog. It may be the guardian of the dead, an ancient spirit of vengeance, or a manifestation of the curse that follows grave-robbers who violate sacred ground. Whatever it is, it obeys laws older than human law and more terrifying than human punishment. It is not an anomaly. It is an inevitability.

The story is also deeply concerned with the theme of decay—not just physical decay, but moral, psychological, and civilizational decay. The protagonists live in a house that is crumbling, surrounded by artifacts of forgotten epochs. They themselves are symbols of cultural exhaustion—men who have no purpose except to experience the sensations of the dead. In this, "The Hound" anticipates Lovecraft's later exploration of decadence in stories like "The Rats in the Walls" and "The Case of Charles Dexter Ward." It suggests that the end of civilization comes not with a bang or an invasion, but with a slow turning inward—an obsession with the past that becomes cannibalistic.

This obsession with antiquity also reflects Lovecraft's personal anxieties. As a writer steeped in classical literature, history, and antiquarianism, Lovecraft often felt alienated from the modern world. His stories are filled with characters who retreat from modernity into ancient books, dead languages, and forgotten ruins. But in "The Hound," he pushes this idea to its grotesque extreme. The protagonists do not merely retreat into the past—they attempt to inhabit it, possess it, consume it. And the past, in return, devours them.

This modern edition has been carefully updated to preserve Lovecraft's lush and immersive language while improving clarity and accessibility for the contemporary reader. Archaic constructions have been smoothed without sacrificing the story's decadent tone, and the pacing has been subtly refined to enhance narrative flow. The original spirit remains untouched—immersive, hallucinatory, and ultimately terrifying.

To read "The Hound" today is to step into a world where horror is not simply about fear—it is about beauty corrupted, about obsession unbound, about the consequences of treating the sacred as spectacle. It is a story that reminds us that the dead are not ours to claim, that the past is not a playground, and that some things, once unearthed, will not return quietly to the grave.

Lovecraft does not offer us a world of moral clarity or redemptive justice. He offers us a world where ancient forces lie in wait, where beauty and horror share the same face, and where those who gaze too deeply into the grave may find it gazing back—with teeth.

Chapter I

My ears won't stop hearing a horrible, nonstop sound—like wings flapping and something far off howling, like a giant dog. I know it's not a dream, and I don't think I'm insane either. Too much has happened for me to hope it's just in my head. St. John is dead—his body torn apart—and only I know why. What I know is so terrifying that I'm ready to take my own life before the same thing happens to me. I feel like something dark and shapeless is chasing me through endless, pitch-black hallways, pushing me closer to the edge.

I hope heaven can forgive the foolishness and obsession that led us down such a terrible path. Bored with our ordinary lives—where even love and adventure became dull—St. John and I threw ourselves into anything that promised to excite or challenge our minds. We explored every strange and artistic movement we could find, but nothing held our interest for long. Eventually, we were drawn to darker and stranger things. We dove deep into the world of Decadent writers and thinkers, but even that wasn't enough unless we kept pushing the limits. After a while, the only thrills we found were through personal, unnatural experiences.

That craving for excitement led us to something I'm ashamed to admit, even now. We became grave robbers.

I can't bring myself to describe what we did in detail, or to list the worst things we collected for our secret museum. We lived together in a big stone house with no servants, and deep underground we built a horrible private room filled with death and horror. We designed it to overwhelm our senses—giant statues of winged demons lit up the room with green and orange lights, and hidden pipes sent out smells to match our moods. Sometimes the room smelled like lilies at a funeral, sometimes like incense from ancient tombs. And sometimes, most horribly, it smelled like fresh graves just dug up.

The walls were lined with display cases. Inside were ancient mummies, stuffed bodies that looked almost alive, and gravestones stolen from the oldest burial grounds on Earth. Some shelves held skulls in every shape and condition—some belonged to famous nobles, others were from newly buried children with golden hair. There were disturbing statues and paintings, some made by St. John and me. One locked book, bound in human skin, held horrifying sketches said to be by Goya—so awful he never dared claim them.

We also had strange musical instruments, and sometimes we played them, creating eerie, twisted sounds that made our skin crawl. Cabinets throughout the room were filled with the most bizarre and disgusting grave goods ever collected. I can't even begin to describe them—but I'm grateful I had the courage to destroy those items before I decided to destroy myself.

The grave-robbing trips we took to collect our disturbing treasures were always planned with great care. We didn't see ourselves as common thieves or monsters—we only went out when the mood, the weather, the season, the setting, and the moonlight felt just right. For us, these moments were a twisted kind of art, and we paid attention to every detail. If the timing felt off, the lighting was wrong, or the digging was clumsy, it would ruin the strange excitement we felt when uncovering some awful secret buried in the earth. We were always chasing new and thrilling places to explore, and St. John was usually the one pushing us forward—until the day he led us to that cursed place where everything finally fell apart.

What strange twist of fate led us to that terrible old graveyard in Holland? I think it was the legends—the stories about a man buried there five hundred years ago. They said he had been a grave robber too, and that he had stolen something powerful from a sacred tomb. I still remember the scene clearly: the pale autumn moon shining over broken gravestones and twisted trees, the grass overgrown and untouched, and huge bats flying across the moonlight. The old, ivy-covered church looked like it was pointing at the sky with a ghostly finger. In one dark corner, glowing insects flickered like little flames of death. The air smelled of rot and something else we couldn't explain, mixed with the breeze coming off faraway swamps and seas. And worst of all, we heard a deep, distant howling—like a massive hound—but we couldn't see anything or tell where it came from. We froze when we heard it, remembering the old stories. They said that the man buried there had been torn apart by a monster centuries ago.

I remembered us digging into that man's grave with our shovels, our hearts racing with a strange mix of fear and excitement. The moon, the shadows, the bats, the trees, and that haunting howl—it all felt like a dream or a nightmare. Then we hit something hard beneath the soil. It was a rotting coffin, crusted with minerals from centuries underground. It was thick and heavy, but we managed to pry it open and look inside.

Surprisingly, a lot of the body had survived the passage of time. Though parts of the skeleton were crushed—likely from the beast that had killed him—it was still mostly whole. We stared in awe at the clean white skull, with its sharp teeth and deep, empty eye sockets. Around the neck bones was a strange amulet, clearly worn by the body. It showed a crouching, winged hound or maybe a sphinx with a dog-like face. It was beautifully carved from green jade in an ancient Eastern style, but its expression was twisted and disturbing. It looked like a mix of death, evil, and animal rage. Along the base was writing we couldn't understand, and on the bottom was a carved symbol— a frightening, grinning skull.

The moment we saw the amulet, we knew we had to have it. Even if we hadn't recognized it, we would have wanted it. But we did recognize it. It wasn't anything normal or known to the world of sane art and history—but we remembered reading about it in the Necronomicon, a forbidden book written by the mad Arab Abdul Alhazred. The book described it as the soul-mark of a corpse-eating cult from the hidden land of Leng in Central Asia. It was said to be a symbol tied to spirits that fed on the dead.

We grabbed the jade amulet, gave one last look at the empty face of the skeleton, and buried the grave again. As we left that terrible place, with the amulet now in St. John's pocket, we thought we saw the bats diving down toward the earth we had disturbed—like they were searching for something unholy. But the moonlight was faint, and we couldn't be sure. The next day, as we sailed away from Holland toward home, we thought we heard that same deep howling again, far in the distance. But the autumn wind was soft and sad, and again—we couldn't be sure.

Chapter II

Less than a week after we returned to England, strange things began to happen. We lived alone, away from people, in a few rooms of an old manor house sitting on a cold, empty moor. We had no friends or servants, and barely anyone ever came to our door. But suddenly, we started noticing strange sounds at night—soft scratching and fumbling around the doors and windows, even on the upper floors. One night, we thought something large blocked the light from the moon at the library window. Another time, we heard a strange whirring or flapping sound nearby. But every time we checked, there was nothing there. We started to think it was all in our heads—maybe our imaginations were still haunted by the soft baying sound we'd thought we'd heard back in the Holland graveyard.

We had placed the jade amulet in a special spot in our private museum and sometimes burned oddly scented candles in front of it. We spent a lot of time reading the Necronomicon by Abdul Alhazred and learning about what the amulet might mean. It talked about the souls of ghouls and their strange connection to the amulet, and what we read started to really disturb us. Then, the fear truly began.

On the night of September 24th, I heard someone knock on my bedroom door. Thinking it was St. John, I told him to come in—but instead of a reply, I heard a high-pitched laugh. When I opened the door, no one was there. I woke St. John, but he said he hadn't left his room and was just as concerned as I was. That same night, the distant howling we'd only imagined before now became real—low, haunting, and terrifying, rolling across the moor.

Four days later, while we were both in the hidden museum, we heard soft scratching at the door that led to the secret staircase. We were frightened—not just of whatever was out there, but also that someone might discover our hidden collection. We quickly turned off the lights and flung the door open, only to feel a strange gust of air rush past us and hear odd sounds fading into the distance—whispers, rustling, and laughter, mixed with words that were definitely being spoken in Dutch. Whether it was a dream or we were truly losing our minds, we didn't know. We only knew we were scared.

From then on, we lived in constant fear, though we were also strangely fascinated. Most of the time we tried to believe we were just going insane from all our strange experiences. But sometimes, we imagined ourselves as victims of something ancient and evil closing in on us. The bizarre things that happened became too many to count. It felt like something evil lived with us in the house. Every night, that awful howling grew louder. On October 29th, we found strange footprints in the dirt beneath the library window—shapes that were impossible to describe. More and more giant bats started circling the house too, something we'd never seen before.

The worst night came on November 18th. St. John was walking home from the faraway train station when something attacked him. It was some kind of terrifying, meat-eating creature that tore him apart. I heard his screams from the house and ran out, only to see a shadowy shape with wings fly off into the moonlight. When I got to him, he was dying. He couldn't speak clearly, but he managed to whisper, "The amulet—that damned thing—" before going still, his body torn and broken.

That night, at midnight, I buried him in one of our overgrown gardens. I whispered one of the dark rituals he had liked so much in life. As I said the final words, I heard the distant howl again—far off on the moor. The moon had risen, but I was too afraid to look at it. When I caught a glimpse of a huge, shadowy shape moving across the moor, I shut my eyes and fell flat on the ground. I don't know how long I lay there, but when I finally got up, shaking, I went back inside and bowed down in fear before the jade amulet we had placed in its shrine.

I was too scared to stay alone in the old house on the moor, so the next day I left for London. I took the jade amulet with me and destroyed the rest of our terrible collection—burning some of it and burying the rest. But after only three nights, I heard the howling again. Within a week, I began to feel like something was watching me in the dark. One evening, while walking along Victoria Embankment to clear my head, I saw a dark shape block the light's reflection in the water. A gust of wind—stronger than the regular night breeze—rushed past me, and I knew that what happened to St. John would soon happen to me.

The next day, I wrapped up the green jade amulet and sailed to Holland. I didn't know if returning it to its original owner would save me, but it seemed like the only logical thing left to try. I still didn't know what the hound really was or why it was after me, but I had first heard it in that old graveyard, and everything that followed—especially St. John's dying words—seemed tied to us stealing the amulet. So when I found out, while staying at an inn in Rotterdam, that it had been stolen from me, I sank into complete hopelessness.

That night the baying grew louder, and the next morning I read about a horrible event in one of the city's worst neighborhoods. People there were terrified. A crime worse than anything they'd ever seen had taken place. A whole family had been torn apart by something unknown, leaving no clues. Neighbors said that all night, above the usual noise of drunk voices, they had heard a deep, eerie sound—like a giant hound's howl.

At last, I returned to the awful graveyard. The pale winter moon cast creepy shadows, and the dead trees drooped over dry, frozen grass and cracked tombstones. The ivy-covered church loomed over everything, pointing its old spire toward the gray sky. The wind screamed over the icy swamps and seas. The baying sound was faint now, and finally stopped as I neared the old grave we had disturbed. A swarm of huge bats hovered there, flying away as I approached.

I don't know why I came back—maybe to pray, or to beg the thing in the grave for forgiveness. Whatever the reason, I began digging with a desperate energy that didn't feel fully like my own. The frozen ground gave way more easily than I expected. But at one point, a thin vulture flew down and tried to claw at the dirt. I struck it with my shovel and killed it. Eventually, I reached the old coffin and pried off its damp, crusted lid. What I saw next was the last thing I ever truly understood.

Inside that ancient box, surrounded by huge, sleeping bats, was the same skeleton we had stolen from—but now it was different. It wasn't clean and still like before. It was smeared with dried blood and bits of torn flesh and hair. Its empty eyes glowed with a sick light, and its twisted mouth was full of sharp red-stained teeth. It grinned at me, almost alive, mocking my fate. Then, from those jaws, it let out a deep howl—like a monstrous dog—and I saw the jade amulet clutched in its filthy claw.

That's when I lost my mind. I screamed and ran, my cries turning into wild, crazy laughter.

Now I know that madness rides the night winds… with teeth and claws sharpened on dead flesh… bringing death while flying on swarms of bats from ruined, ancient temples. And now, as the howling of that rotting monster grows louder, and the flapping of bat wings comes closer, I know I have only one escape left I will use my gun to find the only peace that remains—for there is no other way to escape what cannot be named.

The End

Thank You for Reading

Dear Reader,

We hope this timeless classic has sparked your imagination and enriched your literary journey. Now that you've turned the final page, we want to share a vision for the future of reading—one where every classic you've ever wanted to explore is at your fingertips, in a format that best suits your life.

We'd like to invite you to gain immediate, unlimited digital & audiobook access to hundreds of the most treasured literary classics ever written—along with the option to secure deluxe paperback, hardcover & box set editions at printing cost. Together, we can spark a new global literary renaissance alongside our small, independent publishing house called "The Library of Alexandria."

Thousands of years ago, the Library of Alexandria stood as a beacon of knowledge—until it was lost to history. We aim to reignite that spirit of preservation and discovery right now, in the modern age—only this time, it's accessible to all, in every language and every format.

Picture a world where every timeless classic, novel, poem, or philosophical treatise is not only available to read but also updated for today's readers—modernized, translated into any language or dialect, and ready to enjoy in any format you choose, whether that is in an eBook, audiobook, paperback, or deluxe hardcover & box set version a printing cost.

By joining our movement to rebuild the modern Library of Alexandria, you become part of an unprecedented mission to offer:

- **Unlimited Audiobook & eBook Access to the Greatest Classics of All Time**

  Instantly explore thousands of legendary works, from Plato and Shakespeare to Jane Austen and Leo Tolstoy. All are instantly ready to read or listen to, giving you a complete literary universe at your fingertips.

- **Paperback & Deluxe Editions at Printing Costs:**

  Purchase any title in a paperback, deluxe hardbound, or deluxe boxset edition at printing costs, shipped right to your doorstep. Curate your personal library of Alexandria with editions worthy of display—crafted to last, designed to captivate, and delivered straight to your door.

- **Modern translations for Contemporary Readers in all languages and dialects**

  Discover a vast selection of classics reimagined in clear, current language—no more struggling with outdated phrases or obscure references. Next to the original versions, we aim to offer translations in as many languages and dialects as possible.

  As we continue our translation efforts and add new languages, readers everywhere can connect with these works as if they were written today. By bridging linguistic divides, you're contributing to ensuring that these timeless stories become more meaningful, accessible, and inspiring for people across the globe.

- **Your Personal Library of Alexandria:**

  Over the months and years, you'll curate a unique physical archive of classics—each volume a testament to your taste, curiosity, and love of knowledge. It's not just about owning books—it's about curating a cultural legacy you'll cherish and pass down for generations to come.

- **Join a Global Literary Renaissance:**

  Your support fuels an ongoing mission: allowing us to reinvest in offering deluxe print editions (including special boxsets) at their true cost,

Visit:

www.libraryofalexandria.com

Or scan the code below:

broaden the range of available formats and translations, and extend the reach of these works to new audiences worldwide. By joining today, you're not just preserving a legacy of masterpieces; you set in motion a powerful wave of literary accessibility.

We are more than a publisher—we're a movement, and we can't do it alone. Your support lets us scale our mission, preserving and reimagining history's greatest works for tomorrow's readers.

Become a Torchbearer of knowledge.

Thank you for picking up this book and allowing us into your literary journey. As you turn the pages, know that you're part of something larger: a global effort to keep these stories alive, share their wisdom across borders and generations, and spark a true cultural revival for the modern era.

If this resonates with you—please consider taking the next step by visiting:

www.libraryofalexandria.com

With gratitude and a shared love of knowledge,

The Modern Library of Alexandria Team